NETTIE'S TRIP SOUTH

Ann Turner

NETTIE'S TRIP SOUTH

Illustrated by

Ronald Himler

Macmillan Publishing Company   New York

This story is inspired by my great-grandmother Henrietta's (Nettie's) diary of her trip South, taken in 1859 when she was a young woman. There, she witnessed a slave auction and returned home a committed abolitionist. As she said in her own words, "All I have heard of slavery seemed unreal until now that I *see* for myself."

Text copyright © 1987 by Ann Turner
Illustrations copyright © 1987 by Ronald Himler
Macmillan Publishing Company
866 Third Avenue, New York, NY 10022
Collier Macmillan Canada, Inc.
First Edition
Printed in the United States of America

10 9 8 7 6 5 4 3 2 1

The text of this book is set in 12 point Trump.
The illustrations are rendered in pencil.
Library of Congress Cataloging-in-Publication Data
Turner, Ann Warren. Nettie's trip South.
Summary: A ten-year-old northern girl encounters the ugly realities of slavery when she visits Richmond, Virginia, and sees a slave auction.
[1. Slavery—Fiction] I. Himler, Ronald, ill. II. Title.
PZ7.T8535Ne 1987   [Fic]   86-18135
ISBN 0-02-789240-9

To my dear Aunt Henrietta,
granddaughter of the real Nettie.

—A.T.

Dear Addie, You said, "Tell me about
your trip South; tell me everything."
If we sat in our apple tree
and I told you all,
we would be there 'til the sun set.
But these are the things I remember most;
and though I'm only ten,
I saw the slaves, I saw the South.

Mother and Father waved good-bye,
the buggy creaked, I in my new furs
too excited to cry,
and Sister Julia, grown-up at fourteen.
Brother Lockwood shouted directions
and orders, excited to be
on his first newspaper story.
Father said, "Go, all of you:
War may come soon,
and this is your chance to see the South."

I admit I jumped.
I admit I screamed—a little
when the train chuffed and puffed and hooted
into the station,
my first train ride ever.
Lockwood sat back and pretended to be calm
but Julia and I bounced and twittered
until our lace collars scratched our chins.

Addie, I was so worried I was almost sick.
Julia told me slaves are thought to be
three-fifths of a person. It's in the Constitution.
I'd never seen a slave and wondered,
What were they missing?
Was it an arm, a leg, a foot, or something inside?

I couldn't ask Lockwood,
he has such a sharp tongue,
and Julia was busy being grown-up,
so I kept my worry to myself
all the way south on the train,
across Chesapeake Bay.
I looked and looked at black people,
but I could not see what was missing.

I stayed in my first hotel in Richmond.
I asked our black maid, "Are you a slave?"
She nodded and said, "Tabitha's my name—
don't have no other." Like a cat or a dog,
Addie, with only one name.
I looked and looked,
but she had a nose, two eyes, a mouth,
two arms and, though I could not see her legs,
I saw her feet under her skirts.
I sighed then and Tabitha opened the windows;
a sweet cedar smell rushed in.
She sniffed and said,
"That's the smell of the South, missy."

Next day, Brother took us on a buggy ride
to a near plantation.
Trees were like old men with tattered gray coats,
and the sun pressed down
on our heads. Sister Julia was thirsty
and asked a boy for water.
His face was so black and round and fierce,
it could've been fired from a cannon in war.
I saw where he got the water.
There was a shack run-down
with heaps of rags in the corner,
I think for beds,
and a grandfather with his legs every whichway
lying on the rags.
Everyone smiled and nodded 'cept me.
Some animals live better, Addie.

The cedars didn't smell so sweet
that night, and the smell got in my nose
as Brother walked and talked all that week.
On Saturday we went to town
and stopped on a street by a green gate.

A red flag outside said,
"Negroe Auction Today."
I didn't want to go, Addie,
but Brother said he had to see it
for his story, pulled us in, and sat us down.

There was a platform.
There was a fat man in a tight white suit.
There was a black woman on the platform.
"Jump, aunt, jump!" the man shouted.
Someone called out a price
and she was gone. *Gone*, Addie,
like a sack of flour pushed
across a store counter.

There was a man with a face like the oak
in our yard, all twisted,
and he ran and jumped and was sold.
And two children our age
clasped hands but were bought by different men,
and the man in the white hat
had to tear them apart.

I threw up, Addie, right there
with all the men and ladies about.
They stepped aside and put their handkerchiefs
to their noses. I wanted to cry,
"I'm not what smells!"
But Brother took us home,
walked so fast I knew he was mad.

He made me lie down to rest
while he and Julia packed our bags.
I heard him say, "I've seen all I *need* to see!"
We left, then, the sweet cedar smell
still blowing in the wind,
the sun like a warm hand,
and Tabitha waved from the doorway
and told me to wear my furs.

Addie, I couldn't wear my lace collar,
I felt so raw and ill. We came home
to the white and the ice.
Julia won't talk of what we saw
but Brother makes up for that.
When you come in June
we will climb the apple tree to our perch
and I will tell you all I saw.

Addie, I can't get this out of my thoughts:
If we slipped into a black skin
like a tight coat,
everything would change.
No one would call us by our last names,
for we would not have them.
Addie and Nettie we'd be,
until we were worn out and died.
When someone called, we'd jump!

We could not read in the apple tree
with the sun coming through the leaves,
for no one would teach us to read
and no one would give us a book.

And Addie, at any time we could be sold
by a fat man in a white hat
in a tight white suit
and we'd have to go, just like that.

Dear Addie, Write soon, I miss you,
and I have bad dreams at night.
Love, Nettie.

E   copy 1
Tu

Turner, Ann
   Nettie's Trip South

DEMCO